Cats, Dogs & Sisters

Eleanor Watkins

Illustrated by Pat Murray

By the same author:
Who invented sisters?
The Vicarage Rats

Copyright © Eleanor Watkins 2003
First published 2003
ISBN 1 85999 673 6

Scripture Union, 207–209 Queensway, Bletchley,
Milton Keynes, MK2 2EB, England.
Email: info@scriptureunion.org.uk
Website: www.scriptureunion.org.uk

Scripture Union Australia
Locked Bag 2, Central Coast Business Centre, NSW 2252
Website: www.su.org.au

Scripture Union USA
PO Box 987, Valley Forge, PA 19482
Website: www.scriptureunion.org

The right of Eleanor Watkins to be identified as author of this work has been
asserted by her in accordance with the Copyright, Designs and Patents Act 1988.

British Library Cataloguing-in-Publication Data.
A catalogue record of this book is available from the British Library.

Printed and bound in Great Britain by Creative Print and Design (Wales)
Ebbw Vale.

Cover design: Paul Airy
Cover illustration: Pat Murray

Scripture Union is an international Christian charity working with
churches in more than 130 countries, providing resources to bring the
good news about Jesus Christ to children, young people and families and
to encourage them to develop spiritually through the Bible and prayer.

As well as our network of volunteers, staff and associates who run
holidays, church-based events and school Christian groups, we produce a
wide range of publications and support those who use our resources
through training programmes.

Chapter One

"Jack, don't stuff your food in like that!" said Megan. "Mum, tell him!"

"Eat properly, Jack," said Mum, who was pouring cups of tea.

"I am!" said Jack indignantly. That was just like Megan, and all his sisters for that matter. They bossed him about, were mean to him and got him into trouble. No one deserved to have four older sisters. Especially bossy ones.

It was teatime, and all the family were together, sitting round the table and chattering like magpies. At least, all the girls were chattering. Sometimes their

voices rose to a shriek when two or more
wanted to speak at the same time. Jack
kept on eating his cauliflower cheese, not
listening to them. He was trying to decide
whether or not to go to William's house

to play on his computer. It was quiet at William's.

"But they're so sweet!" Rosie was saying, waving her fork in the air. "Pretty little faces, and blue eyes, and cute whiskers..."

Jack looked at her in amazement. Who on earth could Rosie be talking about? None of her friends, boys or girls, looked like that.

"Close your mouth, Jack," said Amy, the oldest girl. She went on, "I agree with Rosie. I went to look today, and there's a grey one, and a black one with little white paws. They're so tiny – they'd be no trouble at all."

Jack remembered that Rosie had a Saturday job at the pet shop in town. He used to really like that shop, until the day he'd met a very bad-tempered parrot there. Rosie and Amy were talking about kittens!

"We always said we'd get pets some time," said Amy.

"But they have to be looked after," said Mum. "Kittens grow into cats, and sometimes they *are* a lot of trouble."

"But we'd all help. And these two really need a home. The manager says so. They're free to a good home."

"But cat food costs money," said Dad.

"Mind you, I've always rather fancied having a cat," said Mum thoughtfully.

Amy and Rosie looked at each other, and so did Megan and her twin Marianne.

"We could all chip in a bit of our pocket money," said Marianne eagerly.

"Oh, please Dad!" said both the twins together.

Dad could see that he was fighting a losing battle. He said, "Well, I suppose it would be nice to have a cat. Or even two. What do you think, Jack?"

Jack always felt important when Dad or Mum asked his opinion. But the girls nearly always told him what to do, say and think.

He thought now, long and carefully, chewing and swallowing his last mouthful. Then he said, "I'd rather have a dog."

Of course, all the girls jumped down his throat for saying he wanted a dog.

"Jack, you're just being awkward!"

"He does it on purpose!"

"What have you got against kittens?"

"Sweet little things – they never did any harm to anyone!"

Jack sighed. It was no use trying to explain that he had nothing at all against kittens. He quite liked cats, in fact. He wouldn't mind having them at all. But his opinion had been asked for, and he'd given it.

"I'd just rather have a dog," he repeated.

It was true. He'd often thought how good it would be to have a dog of his own. Especially just lately, since William had moved house and he had to go through the car park to get to his new place. He could imagine the dog walking with him, and the kind of dog it would be. Big and black, a Labrador maybe, or a German shepherd. It would stay close to him, and no one would dare to try and make trouble when they came along, him and his dog.

There had been trouble just lately. Some bigger boys from school sometimes hung about the car park, kicking a football or just messing about. They hadn't noticed him much, until one day Megan and Marianne had walked with him to William's house. The boys had seen him and had laughed at him for walking with girls, and now they teased him all the time when he was alone, calling him a wimp and other stupid names. They'd started to pick on him at school, too. He tried to take no notice but sometimes it was hard. He was starting to get frightened.

The following Saturday, Rosie brought home the kittens in a cardboard box. One was grey and fluffy, the other black and shiny with white socks and a white bib. Both had small spiky tails, white whiskers and tiny pink tongues. They mewed in squeaky little voices, and their eyes were wide and blue. The girls made them feel at home in a comfortable box in the kitchen.

At first, everyone fought about whose turn it was to feed and cuddle the kittens. Even Mum and Dad seemed to like them. By Monday morning, they'd settled in and were beginning to explore, padding round in a wobbly kind of way.

Monday mornings were always hectic. Upstairs, two of the girls were arguing. Rosie rushed past on her way downstairs, a hairdryer in her hand. "Jack, be a darling and feed the kittens," she called

over her shoulder, and disappeared into
the downstairs cloakroom. Jack knew it
wasn't really his turn, but he didn't mind.
He poured out the milk and spooned the
kitten food into bowls. The kittens ate it
hungrily and then sat washing their
whiskers. He sat down on the floor and
started stroking the grey one. It lazily

turned its head and licked his fingers with
a tiny rough tongue. The black one
wobbled over and rubbed its face against
Jack's knee, and it began to purr in a
squeaky way. Both of them rolled over

and over and swatted at his fingers as he played with them.

"Jack! Get your shoes on!" called Mum from upstairs.

"I have to go," Jack told the kittens. "But I'll see you later."

He was glad that Rosie had brought the kittens home. He loved them already, and couldn't imagine life without them.

But he still wished he had a dog.

Chapter Two

That morning, they had to walk to school, because Dad needed the car for work. The girls had all gone off to catch the high school bus.

Halfway there, Jack noticed that Charlie and Daz, two of the boys who teased him, were also heading for the short cut between the houses. Jack hung back.

"Come along Jack, don't dawdle," said Mum.

"Couldn't we go the other way?" asked Jack.

"Whatever for? This way is much quicker," said Mum.

Jack saw that Charlie and Daz had noticed him too. They wouldn't make any real trouble with Mum there, but they were grinning and whispering together. He kept his head down and marched ahead of Mum. "Jack," she said, "you're going too fast for me now. What's got into you today? Is something the matter?"

Jack shook his head. He wasn't going to tell tales. That would only make things worse. Charlie and Daz had caught up and were passing them by.

"Mummy's boy!" said Daz in a low voice, and both of them laughed. Jack's face went red.

"Are they friends of yours?" asked Mum.

Jack shook his head. If only a big dog had been walking with them, Charlie and Daz wouldn't have dared to laugh at him. "I wish I had a dog," he said.

"I didn't know you were so keen on dogs," said Mum. "I thought you liked the kittens. Have you and the girls thought of names for them yet?"

The girls had thought of plenty of names over the weekend. Silly names like Pansy and Poppy, Paddypaws and Pussykins. They'd argued all weekend about names, and still hadn't decided. No one had asked Jack's opinion, and probably wouldn't have taken any notice of what he said anyway. He knew what he'd call his dog, though, if he ever got one. Fangs. He'd watched a video with a dog in it called Fangs, and thought it sounded very brave and fearless. No one, not even Daz and Charlie, would dare to have a go at him if he had a dog called Fangs.

The phone rang soon after Jack got home from school that afternoon. Mum answered it. Jack was sitting on the sofa with the kittens, eating his jam sandwich as usual and enjoying the peace, which wouldn't last long when his sisters' bus came in.

Mum was smiling when she put down the phone. "Jack," she said. "I have a job for you. Don't worry – it's one you'll enjoy."

"Is it doing something for Grandma?" he asked.

"No," said Mum. "It's for Mrs Windsmoor, next door but one. She's hurt her ankle and she needs to rest it for a day or two. She asked if one of you could exercise her dog. I thought that as you're so keen on dogs at the moment it would be just the thing for you."

Jack pulled a face. "Oh no! Couldn't one of the girls go?"

"Well, I must say I'm surprised at you," said Mum. "You've been going on about dogs for days. I thought you'd jump at the chance. Anyway, the girls have homework and music practise and aerobics. I said you'd be delighted to help, and that you'd be round after tea to walk Milly."

Jack groaned, and buried his face in the sofa cushions. If there was one dog in the world he didn't want to be seen with, it was Mrs Windsmoor's Milly.

Mrs Windsmoor was waiting for him, with her foot up on a stool and the dog lead in her hand, when Jack went round later. Milly was lying on the rug. She raised her head and looked at Jack as he came in. Milly was a basset hound, with long droopy ears, sad eyes, and looking like going out was the last thing she wanted to do. She was elderly, and fat, and had a long body and short stubby legs.

"It's kind of you, Jack dear," said Mrs Windsmoor. "Milly does need regular exercise. She's put on weight lately, and I do want her to keep fit. Come here, Milly dear, and get your lead on."

Milly heaved herself onto her short legs, looking at Jack as if it was his fault she had to go out. Her tail drooped sadly. Jack knew that she didn't want to go out with him any more than he wanted to take her. Mrs Windsmoor clipped the lead to her collar.

"Have a lovely walk!"

Jack decided he'd have to keep away from places like the recreation ground or the car park in case he was seen out with Milly. It would be awful if any of the boys from school saw him, especially Daz and Charlie. He pulled up his sweatshirt hood and kept his head down, walking

along towards the bungalows where
mostly older people lived.

Just the same, it was very embarrassing.
Milly waddled along
slowly, puffing
and blowing.

Every few metres she sat down and
looked sadly at Jack, as if to say 'Haven't
we gone far enough?' She sighed and
wheezed when he made her get up and go
on again. "I don't like this much, either,"
he told her.

When they reached the seat by the
flower beds, he gave up and sat down.
Milly sank down with a groan and looked
gratefully at him. She leaned her head

against his knee and licked his fingers with a long tongue. He stroked her long brown ears and scratched behind them, feeling sorry for her. It wasn't her fault that she was such a sad old dog.

They sat there until Jack thought that it was long enough and then went slowly home.

"What a nice long walk you've had," said Mrs Windsmoor. "Milly's looking much better for it."

She gave Jack a pound coin, and asked if he'd come again tomorrow, as her ankle was still a bit stiff. Jack was glad of the money, but thought he'd pray especially hard for Mrs Windsmoor's ankle when he went to bed that night.

Chapter Three

Next afternoon, there was another phone call from Mrs Windsmoor. Jack tried to make himself invisible. But it wasn't what he'd thought.

"You don't have to walk Milly this evening," said Mum. "She's ill. Mrs Windsmoor's quite worried about her. She's calling the vet."

Jack felt relieved at first, but then he started to feel guilty. He'd prayed very hard that he wouldn't have to take Milly out again. Mum and Dad always said that God sometimes answered prayer in unexpected ways. Would God make Milly be ill, because of his prayers?

"Is she going to die?" he asked.

Mum hesitated, as though she didn't quite know how to answer. Then she said, "Well, we'll hope not. But remember, Jack, Milly is an old dog. Dogs don't live as long as people so it's possible she might die. You must try not to be too upset if that happens."

Jack went upstairs and sat on his bed. He felt guilty and mean because of the way he'd been about Milly. She couldn't help being old and fat and slow. And now she was sick and might die. He squeezed his eyes tight shut, but a tear managed to slip through. "I didn't mean it, God," he whispered. "I didn't want her to be sick. I'll take her for walks if I have to. Please don't let her die. Please."

All of them saw the vet's Range Rover drive up while they were having tea. It turned into Mrs Windsmoor's drive and was there for quite a long time. Jack hardly dared to look. When the vet had gone, Dad said he'd go round and see if there was anything he could do. He and Mum gave each other a look, the kind of look that meant there were things they didn't want to talk about in front of the children. Upsetting things, like a dog who had died and needed to be buried. Jack felt sick all of a sudden and couldn't finish his tea.

"Are you all right, Jack?" asked Mum. "You look a bit pale."

"I expect he ate too much chocolate after school," said Marianne.

Jack hadn't the heart even to give Marianne a kick under the table. It wouldn't have made him feel better anyway.

Mum was worried about Jack and made him go to bed early. Dad wasn't back from Mrs Windsmoor's, yet.

"Is something bothering you, Jack?" asked Mum.

Jack almost told her everything. But he couldn't quite.

He said, "Mum, what does God do if we pray for something and then we wish we hadn't, because it didn't come out right and we wouldn't have prayed it if we'd known?"

Mum smiled. "That sounds a bit complicated. But it does say in the Bible that Jesus himself helps us when we pray. He helps to sort out what we're trying to say. And he knows what we really mean in our hearts, and why. And God knows just the right way to answer."

Jack's breath came out in a sigh of relief. Maybe God would understand and sort it all out.

"Is Dad back yet?" he asked.

Before Mum had time to answer, they heard the front door open and close and Dad's voice calling, "Anyone about?"

He sounded loud and cheerful, not at all the way you'd sound if you'd just been burying a dead dog. Mum went downstairs, and Jack got out of bed and hurried to the top of the stairs. Dad was laughing.

"You'll never guess! Milly's had pups! Five of them! Mrs Windsmoor's in a real panic. She didn't know Milly was pregnant! She's running round in circles sorting everything out – it's a good thing her ankle's much better!"

Mum laughed too. "Fancy that! No wonder Milly was so fat, and tired all the time! Do you hear that, Jack? Milly's had puppies!"

Jack came down two steps. "Are you sure? Milly's not dead?"

"Sure as anything. Saw them myself. Little fat squeaky things. And Milly's very much alive. I've been helping to get the bedding sorted out, and a place for them to sleep. I'll take you round to see them tomorrow."

Jack felt as though a great weight had been lifted from his shoulders. He came the rest of the way down the stairs. "Could I have something to eat, Mum?"

"I thought you were feeling sick."

"I'm feeling fine now," said Jack.

Dad took Jack round the next day to see the puppies. Rosie went with them, as she considered herself something of an expert on animals now she worked at the pet shop. She went over to examine the puppies as though she was a vet.

They lay on a soft woollen blanket in a large cardboard box with one side removed, a shining, twitching heap of

small plump bodies, fast asleep. Most of
them seemed to be brown and white like
their mother, but one was mostly white
with only small brown patches. Milly lay
nearby, stretched out, looking rather
pleased with herself, though slightly
astonished. Mrs Windsmoor seemed
rather astonished herself. She said, "I had
no idea she was expecting puppies! It's
years and years since her last litter. It's
been quite a shock!"

"I can imagine," said Dad. "They look
nice and healthy though. You should
easily find homes for them."

"I do hope so," said Mrs Windsmoor.
"I don't want six dogs on my hands,

though they are rather sweet. Would you like to hold one, Jack?"

Milly looked anxiously at Jack as he picked up one of the puppies. It felt very warm, velvety soft and quite heavy in his hands. It made little snuffling sounds, as though it didn't really want to be disturbed from sleep just then. He stroked it for a moment and then put it carefully back. Milly heaved a sigh of relief. Having a family of five had been a surprise to her, but she meant to take great care of them.

They said goodbye to Mrs Windsmoor and her extended family and walked home.

"Any ideas about their pedigree?" asked Dad.

"Not really," said Rosie. "Most of them have Milly's colouring. But their legs are longer than a basset's. They'll probably turn out bigger than her. And they're all boys, except the one Jack picked up."

"I thought that one was a boy too," said Jack.

"What would you know?" said Rosie.

Jack didn't quite know how to reply to that, so he said nothing. Rosie was so clever at anything to do with animals. When Rosie was a real vet, he would definitely ask her advice if his dog was ill. He was sure he'd have his own dog by then.

Chapter Four

Jack was walking home from William's house. The days were getting longer now, and the weather was warmer. He didn't mind walking home by himself so much when it was still broad daylight. Plenty of people were about, walking dogs or admiring the spring flowers. He was sure Charlie and Daz wouldn't try anything when there were grown-ups around.

He was wrong. Crossing the car park, he saw them near the pay ticket machine. Charlie and Daz were there, with three other boys – Brent, Harry and Tom, kicking a ball about. As Jack came up, the ball bumped against a red car, and the driver, who'd just got in, wound down her window and yelled at them. "Why don't you go and play in the recreation ground? That's the proper place for footballs!"

She drove away crossly. The boys pulled faces and stuck out their tongues at the back of the car. Charlie bounced the ball up and down. Then he saw Jack.

"Hey, there's the wimp! Hi, wimp, where are you going?"

Jack didn't answer. He tried to hurry past, but the five boys spread out and blocked his path. "I asked you a question, wimp!"

"I'm going home," said Jack. His heart thumped hard.

"Going home to Mummy," sneered Daz. "That's a good little boy!"

Daz grabbed the ball from Charlie and bounced it in Jack's face. It hit his nose and brought tears to his eyes. The boys laughed.

Then, suddenly, they stopped. Someone had come up behind Jack. A tall figure stepped out in front of the boys. "Clear off, you lot! Go and play somewhere else."

The five boys suddenly looked much smaller. They stared at the tall person as though they'd like to answer him back, but they drifted away towards the recreation ground, bouncing the ball between them.

Jack felt his nose to see if it was bleeding. It wasn't. The other person patted his shoulder and said, "All right, mate?"

Jack nodded and looked up into the face of a bigger boy. He was much older and taller than Jack, almost a man really. He had bright blue eyes that were looking out from under the peak of a blue baseball cap, and he was carrying a sports bag. He wore trainers, a sweatshirt and jogging pants, and when he took off his cap to scratch his head, his hair was fair and short. Jack had the strange feeling that he'd seen him before.

"It's Jack, isn't it?" asked the boy, or man, whichever he was. "Amy's brother?"

Jack nodded again, and the boy stuck out his hand. "I'm Sam Walters. From church. I go to the youth group with Amy. And Rosie, and the twins."

Of course. Jack remembered now, but Sam looked different in sports clothes, with a cap on.

"Those losers giving you hassle?" asked Sam. "Don't worry, they've gone now. I'll walk home with you if you like."

Jack almost wished that Charlie and Daz and the rest were still there, to see him walking home with Sam, who strode along like a man who wouldn't put up with any nonsense from anybody. Sam talked to him as they walked, telling him about the gym he went to, and the workouts he'd been doing. Jack listened with admiration. Sam was tough.

They reached his front door and stopped. Jack rang the bell, because he'd forgotten to take a key again. Steps pounded down the stairs. Amy opened the door, with her hair flying out round her head, looking cross to be disturbed. "Why don't you remem—" Then she saw Sam, stopped and blushed. "Oh, hello."

Sam grinned. "Hi, Amy. I just walked home with Jack."

Jack hoped that Sam wasn't going to say that he was being hassled. He didn't want any of his sisters to know. It wasn't that they'd laugh at him, because he knew they wouldn't. They might be horrid to him but they never let anyone else treat him badly. In fact, they would probably all want to go and sort out the bullies right away. That would make things much worse, being defended by a bunch of girls. He'd never hear the last of it.

But Sam didn't say a word about what had happened in the car park. Instead, he just grinned at Amy in a soppy kind of way. She was grinning back, her cheeks pink and shiny. Then she said, "Thanks. Er – would you like to come in for a coffee?"

"Thanks very much," said Sam, and stepped inside at once. He put down his sports bag in the hall, along with all the hockey sticks and roller blades. Music blared from upstairs. Marianne stuck her head out from the kitchen and said, "Oh, hi!" Mum was upstairs putting ironing away and Dad was at the computer in the study. But there was no one in the sitting room. Sam sat on the sofa and took off his cap. He ran his fingers through his short fair hair, making it stand up. Jack sat down next to him.

"You like sport, Jack?"

Jack nodded. "Yes, especially football. But not with that lot. They don't play fair."

"Losers," agreed Sam. "Tell you what. Maybe you and I could have a kick around sometime. I'm a qualified coach."

Jack thought that would be great. A real football coach, almost grown-up, playing with him. He hoped the other boys would notice. It was almost better than having a big dog of his own. "Could William come too?" he asked, and Sam nodded and said, "Course he can."

Amy came in with mugs of coffee on a little tray. There were only two mugs. Jack noticed that she'd quickly brushed her hair and put some of the nicest chocolate biscuits on a plate, and brown sugar lumps in a glass bowl. Amy glared at him. "Isn't it your bedtime, Jack?"

"Not yet. Guess what, Amy? Sam's going to coach me in football!"

"It's very kind of him to take the trouble," said Amy. "One lump or two, Sam?"

"Three, please," said Sam, and grinned. Amy handed a mug to Sam and sat opposite.

"Jack," said Amy. "I think I heard Mum calling you."

Jack hadn't heard anything. But the way Amy was glaring at him, he had the feeling she wanted him to make himself scarce. It wasn't fair, because Sam was his friend after all, not hers.

But just then Mum did call from upstairs, and they all heard. He pulled a face at Amy, said goodnight to Sam and helped himself to a lump of sugar from the bowl as he went past.

Chapter Five

The kittens now had official names –
they were called Pip and Squeak. Jack
thought these names were a bit silly, but
not as silly as some that had been
suggested. They were growing fast and
getting into everything. They climbed up
curtains and sharpened their claws on
armchairs, they scrambled onto
sideboards and table tops, knocking over
small ornaments. They had a basket in
the kitchen, but quite often one or the
other of them would sneak upstairs and
find a soft spot on someone's bed. Jack
and the girls often let them stay there all

night, and would be woken in the morning by a soft paw patting their cheeks, or even four feet walking across their faces. Dad said that when they were a bit bigger and able to look out for themselves, he'd make a cat flap in the back door. Then the kittens could get in and out by themselves and give everyone a bit of peace.

The following Friday, Sam came round to pick up Jack and take him for some football practise. Amy was there to open the door to him, all dressed up in a purple top Jack hadn't seen before, and her hair smooth and shiny in a new style. Sam noticed it at once.

"I like your hair like that," he said.

Amy looked pleased and blushed. "Thank you," she said. "See you later, then."

They went off to the recreation ground, with Sam bouncing the ball between them.

"You're lucky having such a pretty sister," he said.

"Which one do you mean?" asked Jack.

"Well – all of them," said Sam quickly. "You're lucky."

Jack almost said, "I don't think so!", but then he remembered that although the girls were mean to him a lot of the time, now and then they surprised him by being nice. Like when Megan had let him use her art supplies for his painting project, and even helped him with it. Or when Rosie had picked him up after a bad fall from his bike, and hugged him and put a plaster on. Or when he'd gone into town on his own and missed the last bus and they'd all come looking for him.

But he didn't really want to think about his sisters when there was a football at his feet, someone like Sam to coach him, and no bullies to worry about.

Amy was there again when they got in, with coffee ready and her nails freshly painted to match her top. Dad and Mum chatted with Sam, and Jack could see that they liked him too. He went to bed feeling tired from the football practise, but with a good comfortable feeling inside him.

On Sunday morning, Jack looked out for Sam at church. He saw him come in with his parents, a man who looked just like an older version of Sam, and a plump smiling woman. Sam didn't sit with them but stood looking around for a moment.

Sometimes Jack's sisters sat with their friends at the back of the church but today Amy was sitting in a seat all by herself. To his surprise, Sam went and sat down beside her. Jack nudged Marianne, who was sitting next to him. "I want to go and sit with Sam."

"Well, you can't," she hissed.

"Why not? Amy is."

"That's because they're going out together."

"Are they?"

"Of course, silly!"

Mum leant across and whispered, "Be quiet, you two!" Then the service began. Jack wasn't sure what to think. He knew that older boys and girls did go out with each other. He'd never thought Sam would do anything so silly, though. And especially not with Amy, who screeched when she was cross and slammed doors when things weren't going right.

He took a quick look at them when it was time to go out for Children's Church.

Sam and Amy were singing together, sharing a hymn-book. When Amy saw him looking, she stopped singing for a moment and pulled a face at him. He pulled one back. He could tell Sam a thing or two about Amy, and maybe he would, too, if he got the chance.

When they got home for dinner, Jack noticed that Pip, the black kitten, was curled up asleep in the basket, but Squeak was not there.

Everyone began to run around, frantically searching through the whole house. They searched under beds, inside cupboards, and behind the furniture. But there was no sign of a grey kitten.

"Where was he when we left for church?" asked Mum.

No one could think where he'd been. Then Megan remembered that Jack had gone back into the house to get his jacket.

"I bet he got out while the door was open," she said.

Everyone looked at Jack. He felt he was getting the blame again but he couldn't remember if he'd left the door open or not while he went in. There was a really busy road close to their house. If Squeak had escaped, he could have got run over…

Dad put a reassuring hand on his shoulder. "He can't have gone far. Let's spread out. Twins, you go and search the back garden. Amy and Rosie, go and ask Mrs Windsmoor if she's seen or heard anything. Don't worry, Jack."

Jack felt that he had to search too, so he tagged along with Amy and Rosie. Amy looked at his anxious face and said, "Cheer up, Jack. It wasn't your fault he got out."

And Rosie said, "We could say a prayer – God'll help us find him." They did, and Jack felt better.

Mrs Windsmoor opened the door to them. She said she'd been indoors all morning and hadn't noticed anything. Milly came to the door with her. She was looking much thinner than she had been, but just as sad as ever.

"How are the puppies?" asked Rosie.

"Oh, splendid, but a lot of work. Aren't they, Milly?"

Milly agreed with a slight wag of her tail. "We moved them into the shed," said Mrs Windsmoor. "To give us both a break. Would you like to see them?"

Amy and Rosie must have thought it wouldn't be polite to say no, because they all followed Mrs Windsmoor to the garden shed, with Milly waddling along behind them. Jack saw that someone had made a flap in the shed door, like a cat flap, for her to go in and out.

The pups had grown a lot. They lay asleep on a warm blanket bed. They woke up when they heard everyone come in and tumbled towards their mother in an eager jumble of brown and white bodies, demanding food. Milly licked them absentmindedly, but didn't seem to want to feed them just then. Jack sat down beside them and stroked the warm wriggling bodies.

"They've all got names," said Mrs Windsmoor. "That brown one's Bobby. And those two are Sally and Freddie. The biggest one is called Buster. And that little one's Patches. He's a bit shy."

Patches was a little smaller than most of the others. Jack noticed that they seemed to boss him about and push him around. He felt sorry for the pup and gave him a cuddle. "I know what it feels like!" he whispered into the pup's floppy soft ear.

Milly's long droopy ears had pricked up and her brown nose sniffed the air. Then she walked over to a corner of the shed, with her indignant hungry pups toddling after her. There she stopped, sniffing and staring hard at a pile of old sacks.

"There's something there," said Mrs Windsmoor. "What is it, Milly? A mouse?"

At the mention of mice, Amy and Rosie both drew back a little. But Jack had a sudden idea. He went over and pulled back the top sack. Crouching there, spitting with terror, was their small and frightened grey kitten.

Chapter Six

They were seeing much more of Sam these days. Two or three evenings a week he came round, and it wasn't just to play football with Jack. Sometimes he and Amy went to the gym together, or helped each other with homework. If they didn't have homework, they watched a video together.

But every Friday after school, Sam took Jack out with the football to train. Quite often they called for William, and the three of them went across to the recreation ground.

They had dropped off William at his house one Friday and were heading for home across the top of the rec, where the path was lined with flowers and bushes. As they went, they dribbled the ball between them, taking a shot every so often. One of Jack's sent the ball flying into the middle of a huge rhododendron bush.

"Good shot!" said Sam, and dived into the bush to look for the ball. Jack sat down on a bench to get his breath, swinging his legs.

Suddenly, he heard the clatter of feet and boys' voices. The bullies were approaching from the car park, bored and looking for something to do. Jack tried to make himself as small as he could, but they had already seen him. Jack could hear Sam rustling about in the bushes, looking for the ball, but couldn't see him. Neither could the bullies. They thought Jack was all alone.

"Hey, there's the wimp!"

"Let's go and talk to him!"

"What d'you think you're doing wimp?"

Jack felt as though he was glued to the seat. He stopped swinging his legs and said, "Nothing."

The four boys – Charlie, Daz, Brent and Harry – crowded around the bench, surrounding him. Daz pushed his face up close, "Want a fight, Wimpy?"

Jack's heart beat fast, "No."

He wished Sam would hurry up, but he seemed to be having trouble finding the ball. Jack's mouth felt so dry that he couldn't utter another sound.

Daz gave Jack's shoulders a push, and the other boys jeered. "Wimpy's scared! Look at him! He's going to cry in a minute!"

Suddenly there was a shaking in the rhododendrons and Sam emerged, holding the ball and looking surprised.

"What's all this shouting about? What are you lot doing?"

The boys looked at Sam, passing the ball from one hand to another and staring at them with his bright blue eyes – he looked quite scary!

"We're not doing anything."

"What's it got to do with you anyway?"

"We're talking to wimp, that's all."

"We're mates of his."

"His name's Jack," said Sam. "Is that right, Jack? Are they your mates?"

Suddenly, Jack felt his courage return with a rush. Seeing Sam standing there, tall and strong, and the boys looking at him, shuffling their feet and making excuses, he suddenly felt as bold as a lion.

"No," he said. "They're not my mates. They're a bunch of losers, that's what they are."

The boys' eyes widened at this insult, and one or two of them muttered a threat. But they didn't dare do anything with Sam there. Jack got up and stood beside Sam.

"I'd push off, fast, if I were you," Sam told them. "And find something better to do than picking on people. Come on, Jack."

They walked off, leaving the bullies
muttering among themselves.
Jack felt so brave and strong
that it almost made him
dizzy. He just couldn't resist
turning his head, pulling a
horrible face, and calling,
"See you, losers!"

He could hardly believe he'd said that,
and at once he wished he hadn't. He saw
Charlie and Daz make a threatening
gesture behind Sam's back, and Charlie's
face went red as he whispered, "We'll get
you, wimp. You just wait!"

Afterwards, Jack wondered how he'd
ever had the nerve to speak like that to
the bullies. He wished he hadn't.
Grandma always said that words
couldn't be taken back once they were
spoken, and it was true. He'd been brave
for a moment, but now he was scared.
Really scared. Because now they'd be
really out to get him.

He really did need a dog of his own, a big dog, to protect him and give him courage.

"Please could we get a dog?" he asked Dad after he had come back from football, when the two of them were out in the garden.

"I thought you'd changed your mind about that," said Dad.

Jack shook his head. "No. I still want one. I really do."

Dad leaned for a moment on his hoe. "I had a dog when I was your age," he said.

"Ben, his name was. A kind of collie cross. He was a very clever dog, too. Always knew when it was time for me to come home from school. He'd be there, waiting at the garden gate."

Jack's heart leapt. When he got his dog, Fangs, maybe he'd know when Jack got out of school too. Maybe he'd be there every day, waiting. Maybe he'd go with Jack everywhere he went, never let him out of his sight. Maybe...

But there wasn't any dog called Fangs. Jack sighed deeply.

Dad looked at him. "This would really mean a lot to you, wouldn't it?"

Jack nodded. "Yes, Dad."

"It's good for a boy to have a dog," said Dad, thoughtfully. "I don't see why we shouldn't get you one. What with kids and cats already, one more mouth to feed isn't going to make that much difference."

Jack's heart leapt again. "Really, Dad? A real dog?"

"Really and truly," said Dad. "I'll have to talk to Mum, of course. And we'll have to decide what kind of dog. We'll have to get the right one."

Jack felt a big grin come across his face. He knew just what kind of dog they'd get. A big, black, brave one. Called Fangs.

Chapter Seven

Dad must have talked to Mum, and to all the girls too, because at breakfast everyone knew that they were getting a puppy. Everyone had something to say about it too.

"Poodles are sweet," said Amy, whose nails were painted bright blue this morning. "And you can clip them into such lovely shapes."

"So are dachshunds," said Rosie. "One came into the shop last week."

"All on its own?" asked Jack.

"Course not, silly," said Rosie.

"I'd like a spaniel," said Marianne.

"Or a greyhound," said Megan. "It could go running with me."

Jack listened to all these opinions. No one asked him. He knew no one would listen if he said he didn't want a soppy clipped poodle, or a dachshund with silly short legs like Milly's, or even a spaniel or a greyhound. He knew what he wanted, and that was Fangs. Then he caught Dad's eye across the table, and knew it would be all right. Dad hadn't forgotten their conversation.

Rosie came home from the shop at lunch time, bringing with her some telephone numbers of people with puppies for sale. Dad had a look at them.

"I think we could try a couple of these this afternoon," he said.

"Good idea," said Rosie. "I'd come along and advise you, but I have to get back to the shop. But you can ring my mobile if there's anything you want to ask."

Rosie was now so confident in her knowledge of animals that she gave advice whether it was asked for or not.

"I'll have to stay in and get ready this afternoon," said Amy. Jack remembered that she and Sam were going to a concert with the rest of the youth group.

"I can come," said Marianne. "I'm not doing anything."

"Neither am I," said Megan.

Jack sighed. He'd hoped that he and Dad would be going on their own to look at the puppies, but he supposed that two sisters were better than four. Megan and Marianne were having one of their days of doing everything alike. Usually they dressed differently, and had different hairstyles and different friends and different interests. Today, both of them wore identical pink T-shirts, with blue jeans cropped off below the knee and white trainers. Both of them had their hair in pony-tails, fastened by the same silver scrunchie bands, with silver-strapped watches on their left wrists and glittery bangles on their right. Even Mum and Dad had difficulty telling them apart on days like this, but Jack could always tell. They kindly allowed him to sit in the front of the car with Dad.

At the first place they called at, they heard the barking and yapping of dogs even before they rang the doorbell. An elderly woman came to the door, with several dogs running around her feet. There was a cocker spaniel, a kind of terrier, and two others who could have been a mixture of anything. All of them looked anxiously at the visitors.

"Oh yes," said the woman. "I'm Miss Bakewell. Yes, I breed dogs and I have two litters just now. Do come in."

Dogs filled the house and spilled out into the yard and garden at the back. They were shown into a large, dog-filled kitchen. The two mothers were sitting in baskets by a big stove. In front of them a golden-brown sea of puppies rolled and tumbled over the floor and out into the yard beyond.

"Kate and Susan," said Miss Bakewell, introducing the two mothers. "They have eleven puppies between them. All of them are ready for new homes now."

Kate and Susan raised their heads and looked at the visitors in a bored kind of way. They didn't seem at all interested when Jack and the girls stroked and petted the puppies. They didn't seem very interested in the puppies either. The puppies, encouraged by the attention, began to pounce on their feet and nibble at their shoelaces. One of Marianne's came undone, and a pair of puppies began to tug at it, growling squeaky little growls. Megan and Marianne giggled helplessly.

"Now now, you naughty boys, stop that!" said Miss Bakewell, waving at them

with a rolled newspaper. Two of the other
puppies grabbed the paper and began to
rip shreds off. The girls giggled and Jack
couldn't help joining in.

"They're well behaved usually," said
Miss Bakewell, a little flustered. "Excellent
pedigrees."

"I'm sure they have," said Dad.
"They're very nice. But we have others to
see. We'll be in touch."

Jack guessed that meant they probably
wouldn't be having one of these puppies.

He was half glad and half sorry. The little spaniels were plump and cuddly and funny. But he couldn't imagine calling one of them Fangs.

Dad and Miss Bakewell chatted for a few more minutes before they left. Three or four dogs came to see them off, with six or seven puppies scampering behind. The two mothers never moved.

"A bit unruly," said Dad. "Reminded me of home. Any of your shoelace left, Megan?"

"Not much," said one of the twins. "And it's Marianne."

They had time to look at one other litter that afternoon. The owner let them take the dogs out for a run in his field. These puppies were a kind of cross-breed, part collie and part springer spaniel. The pups were black and white, with long legs and small ears. They bounded up to the visitors and jumped up, full of energy, ready for a game. Jack thought they looked good fun and could see that they would grow to be quite big dogs. "Fangs?" he said to one, trying out the name. The young dog put its head on one side and pricked its ears at him. He could see it wanted to be his friend. Was this the one?

"I think I'll give Rosie a buzz and see what she thinks," said Dad, taking out his mobile phone. Jack stroked the friendly pup's ears as Dad talked, and the pup wriggled with joy.

Jack could hear a lot of squawking going on from Rosie's end of the line. Dad had to hold the phone a little away from his ear as Rosie was talking so loud! He put the phone away and looked at Jack and the twins. "Won't do, I'm afraid. Rosie says this kind of crossbreed is trouble. She knows of someone who had a dog like this and it chased sheep. The collie in them is attracted to sheep, you see, and the spaniel part is a hunting dog. They'll chase sheep and maybe other animals too. Maybe cats. We don't want trouble, so we'd better not go for one of these."

This time Jack was more sorry than glad. He liked the black and white dog. Trust Rosie to go and spoil everything. He'd tell her what he thought when he saw her.

But, driving home, he stopped feeling cross and just felt sad instead. He still hadn't found his dog.

Chapter Eight

The next day was hot. In another couple of weeks, school would be over for the summer and the long holidays would be here. The weather was so nice that Mum and Dad decided it was a waste to spend any of it cooking and eating indoors. They'd have a barbecue lunch after church.

After Children's Church, Jack went to speak to the leader, Jo. There was a question he wanted to ask.

"Jo," he said, "does God always hear our prayers? I mean, every single time?"

"Yes," said Jo. "Every single time. Why do you ask, Jack?"

Jack thought for a moment. God had answered prayers for him, lots and lots of times, in all kinds of ways. Even when he didn't really expect him to. He could think of so many times this had happened. But now he'd been praying and praying, asking for a dog, and he still hadn't got one.

He said, "I don't always get what I ask for. Not every time."

Jo smiled. She said, "Well, you see, God knows everything, and he always wants the best for us. Sometimes what we ask for isn't quite the right thing. Or the best. Or it isn't quite the right time for it to happen."

"Should I stop praying then?" asked Jack.

Jo laughed. "No! Keep on praying, and trust God to answer in the right way, at the right time. You might be surprised at what happens!"

Jack thought about that all the way home. He'd been praying for a dog and he'd keep on praying. But he wished God would hurry up.

The barbecue was a great success. Sam had come to lunch, and he and Dad did all the cooking, starting up the barbecue and

grilling chops and chicken legs. Mum and the girls ran in and out with bowls of salad, baked potatoes, bread rolls, paper towels and plastic plates and cutlery. Mum loved barbecues – there was hardly any washing up.

After they'd eaten, Mum gathered together the bits of chop and chicken and asked Jack to give them to the cats. Pip and Squeak were big now, more cats than kittens. They came and went through the cat flap just as they liked. The two of them were quite different. Pip loved lying in the sun or by a warm fire, snoozing for hours. Squeak, on the other hand, was always wandering. He usually came back by himself, safe and sound, though Jack sometimes worried about him.

Pip lay asleep on the back garden wall, out of the way of the girls and Sam, who had set up a swingball game on the back lawn and were bashing it back and forth, but Squeak was missing again.

"Want a go, Jack?" asked Sam.

"I'll find Squeak first," said Jack, putting down the cats' bowl. He had an idea where to look. Since that first time he'd escaped, as a small kitten, Squeak had often made his way to the next-but-one garden, where for some reason he'd taken a great liking to Milly's pups.

"I'm just going to Mrs Windsmoor's to get Squeak," he told Mum.

"All right," said Mum. "Why don't you stay for a while and see how the pups are doing?"

Jack intended getting back as soon as possible so he could play swingball. He found Squeak right away, curled up in the sun in Mrs Windsmoor's porch with one of the young dogs.

"I never saw anything like it," said Mrs Windsmoor, "the way those two have made friends. They make a beeline for each other the minute that cat comes in through the gate." She stroked the long ears of the young dog. "He's lonely, is Patches, now that all the others have found homes."

"Have they all gone then?" asked Jack.

"Every single one," said Mrs Windsmoor. "The last one, Freddie, went just yesterday. Patches is all alone. Even his mother doesn't want to know him any more."

Milly lay stretched out in the shade, fast asleep and snoring. When Patches got up and ambled over to her, she lifted her head, glared at him and growled. The young dog crept sadly back to the porch.

"Why doesn't she want him any more?" asked Jack.

"That's the way with dogs," said Mrs Windsmoor, "and with most animals. When the pups grow up, the mother doesn't want to know them."

Jack hoped his mother wouldn't be like that when he'd grown up. He felt sorry for the young dog. Patches was tall and gangling, like an awkward teenager. He had large sad basset's eyes, a basset's long droopy ears, and a white coat with dark brown patches but he had long legs. He looked sadly at Jack, and wagged his tail shyly. Jack had picked up Squeak. He put him down again, and Squeak sauntered through the gate and towards home without a backward glance. Patches looked after him and whined a little.

"Never mind," said Mrs Windsmoor. "He'll be back another day."

Jack patted Patches' head and stroked his long velvety ears. Patches put out a long pink tongue and shyly licked Jack's hand.

"He likes you," said Mrs Windsmoor. She paused, and then said, "Tell you what. It was so good of you to take Milly out that time. Would you like to take Patches for a little walk? He's missing his brothers and sister so much."

Jack took his hand away. He didn't want to take Patches out. He said quickly, "Sorry, but I'm expected back home."

"It would be all right," said Mrs Windsmoor. "It was your Mum who suggested you might like to, the other day. I could give her a ring. She wouldn't mind."

Suddenly Jack had a very strange feeling. He could see what was going on here. Mrs Windsmoor, and Mum and Dad, and probably his sisters too, knowing them, were plotting to get him to make friends with Patches.

Patches! Looking at him, Jack felt he was the very last dog in the world he would choose, except perhaps Milly. Patches was young and shy and anxious to please. He wasn't brave and big and bold. He wasn't Fangs. Jack didn't want him.

He looked at the dog's pleading brown eyes and sighed. From his own garden came the sounds of the girls shrieking, Sam laughing and the ball slamming to and fro.

They were having fun. Taking Patches out would be no fun at all.

He sighed again, and said, "All right. I'll take him out. Just for a little while."

Chapter Nine

Jack walked along with Patches on the lead. Patches followed with his head down, as far behind Jack as he could get. His tail was down too and he didn't seem to be enjoying himself at all.

He knows I don't really want him, thought Jack suddenly. Then he thought – but I suppose I could pretend I want him, just for a bit.

"Patches! Come on!" he said, and the young dog lifted his head and wagged his tail a little. His sad brown eyes looked hopeful. "Let's go to the rec," said Jack.

It was busy at the recreation ground –
lots of people were out for Sunday
afternoon walks. Patches sniffed about a
bit but kept his eye on Jack. An old
football lay abandoned by a bench. Jack
anchored Patches' lead to a leg of the
bench and began to kick the ball around.
Patches sat down and watched, his head
on one side. But when the ball rolled near,
he rushed at it.

Jack thought that maybe Patches would
like to play too. He decided to let him off
the lead for a bit. He somehow didn't
think Patches would run away.

He was right. Patches watched the ball
every moment and began to follow it as
soon as he was free. He watched every
move that Jack made. When Jack made a
goal shot between the seat and a holly
bush, Patches dived for the ball on his long
legs, and grabbed it with a twist of his
brown and white body. He put the ball
down at Jack's feet.

"Well saved!" said Jack in admiration.

He gave Patches a pat and tried another shot and another. However the shot came, the dog jumped and plunged, catching the ball every time. His ears flew in all directions, his long legs leaped and his eyes lost their sadness and began to shine.

Jack got hot and out of breath before Patches did. He sat down to rest and cool off. Patches sat beside him, his eyes on Jack, tongue lolling, waiting for him to pick up the ball again. Jack had a happy feeling. Who'd have thought that Patches would turn out to be an ace goalkeeper? He couldn't wait to tell Sam.

Then, suddenly, his heart sank. There were the bullies, coming across the grass towards him, just the way they had that other time. And this time Sam wasn't here. It was just him and Patches.

He looked around in panic, quickly clipping on the dog lead. Not so many people were about now. Most had drifted off towards the pond, to feed the ducks and sit in the shade. He got up and began to walk away towards home.

"Not so fast!" shouted a boy's voice. "I want a word with you!"

Jack kept on walking. But suddenly, they were surrounding him, all five of them. His heart thumped and he hardly dared look at them.

"I want a word with you," repeated Charlie. "You called me some names last time I saw you here. Remember?"

Jack remembered only too well. He wished he hadn't said those things. He'd only been so bold because Sam was there.

"I said I'd get you for that," said Charlie. "I don't take cheek. Not from you, not from anybody. Do I, boys?"

The others all agreed, with a lot of snickering and shoving.

"So, what you got to say, Wimpy?"

Jack found his voice. "Sorry," he said, and he'd never meant anything so much in all his life.

"Sorry isn't good enough," said Charlie with a sneer. "You're gonna have to do something to prove it. Now what shall we make him do, boys?"

There was more sneering and some rude remarks. Jack noticed that one or two of the boys looked uneasy. Brent said, "Oh, come on, Charlie, leave him alone. Let's go and play football."

Then he noticed something else. Patches was terrified of the noisy, shoving gang of boys. He pressed himself up against Jack's legs, trembling.

For a moment Jack felt ashamed of him. If his dog Fangs had been here, he'd have snarled and sent the bullies scattering and running. But Fangs wasn't here. There wasn't any Fangs.

But there was God. God never left him, no matter what was happening. God would take care of him, and he, Jack, would take care of Patches. Help me, God, he prayed silently. Patches is so scared.

Gradually, he felt his own fear drain away. He put his hand on Patches' head and said quietly, "It's all right. I'm here." He felt the dog's quivering grow less. Then he heard his own voice saying, quite loudly, "I said I'm sorry. I shouldn't have called you names that time. Now I'm going home."

He must have looked different too, because Charlie's mouth fell open. Nobody tried to stop Jack. He and Patches walked through the middle of the group of boys. He suddenly realised that most of them were only about his size. If he'd met one on his own they wouldn't have tried to bully him at all. They stuck together because it made them feel better.

Charlie seemed to pull himself together. He said angrily, "You're not getting out of it like that! Let's get him, boys!"

Jack kept walking. He saw out of the corner of his eye that the other boys weren't moving. One of them said, "Shut up, Charlie. Let him go."

Brent's voice said, "His dog's a cool goalie!"

Some sort of scuffle was going on. Jack stopped and turned to look. Charlie had thumped one of the other boys and they'd thumped back. Then Charlie turned and stamped off, looking to see if the others were following. None of them did.

"Hey, Jack!" called Daz. "Can we play football with your dog?"

Jack didn't answer for a moment. He'd been scared by these boys for so long that normally he'd have thought there was a trick in it somewhere. But things were different. Charlie had gone and the others just seemed like ordinary boys. And he wasn't scared any more.

He looked down at Patches, remembering how he loved diving for the ball, and how fast his long legs would go.

"Well, all right, then," he said. "But only a couple of games. We've got to go soon."

Chapter Ten

They were finishing their fourth game, and the side with Patches in goal hadn't lost. No one could score past him!

All of them were hot and thirsty. One of the boys had a can of Coke, which he shared with all of them, including Jack. But Jack knew that he had to get a drink for Patches too.

There was a small fountain near the flower beds. Jack wasn't sure that dogs were meant to drink from it, but nobody said anything when he took Patches for a drink. He'd just finished when Jack heard voices calling his name.

"Jack!"

"Jack, where are you?"

"Ja – ack!"

It was his sisters and Sam, hurrying through the rec in search of him. When they saw him, they descended on him and Patches with shrieks and yells.

"Jack! There you are!"

"Wherever have you been all this time?"

"Mum and Dad were really worried!"

"So was Mrs Windsmoor!"

Jack sighed. He was in for it again. But Patches was really terrified, pressing tight against his legs and quivering.

"You're frightening Patches," he said.
"Don't shout so loud. I was playing
football, that's all."

That set them off again.

"You've been gone HOURS!"

"You're really going to get it!"

Sam looked a bit worried too. But all
he said was, "You all right, mate?"

"Yes," said Jack. "I'm fine."

"I saw those bullies going off with a
football," said Sam. "Was it them you
were playing with?"

Jack nodded. He wanted to explain
everything to Sam, but his sisters were
off again.

"What bullies?"

"Have you been getting bullied, Jack?"

"Why didn't you tell us?"

"We'd have sorted them out!"

"It's okay," said Sam. "I think he's
managed to sort it out for himself. That
right, Jack?"

Jack nodded again. "They're okay
really." And he thought, God helped

me not to be afraid, and I did sort it out. I did.

"Come on, Patches, it's all right," he said, and gave the dog a pat. Patches stopped quivering and followed on the lead, keeping as far as possible from the chattering girls. On the way home, he explained a little of what had happened. But they were late for tea, and had to hurry.

First they had to deliver Patches back to Mrs Windsmoor. Jack wished he didn't have to take him back. He was hoping that Mum, Dad and Mrs Windsmoor would let him keep Patches as his own dog. Because he suddenly realised that all his dreams of a big black dog called Fangs were just that – dreams. There wasn't a dog called Fangs, and never had been. Patches was the dog he really wanted, because Patches was an ace footballer, quick and clever, although he was still young and shy and easily frightened. Patches needed him, to encourage him and help him to grow up. Patches was the dog for him.

But there was a niggling doubt in his mind. What if Mrs Windsmoor really wanted to keep Patches for herself, now that Milly was old? What if she didn't want to let him go?

They'd reached Mrs Windsmoor's house. "Can I just take him in by myself?" he asked and knocked on the door.

"Had a nice time, Jack?" asked Mrs Windsmoor.

"Lovely, thanks," said Jack. He cleared his throat. "Mrs Windsmoor, are you really looking for a home for Patches?"

"Oh yes, dear. I am. We really can't be doing with a young dog about the place at our ages, Milly and I. We like our peace and quiet. Besides, I couldn't keep up with him. He's going to be a big dog when he's fully grown, and will need lots of exercise. It would be very difficult for me. Mind you, I'd want him to go to a good home. And one not too far away, so that we could see him again, now and then."

Jack felt his heart lift. It was going to be all right. He was sure that Mum and Dad would agree to have Patches. In fact, he was pretty sure that they'd already planned it out with Mrs Windsmoor. And maybe God had planned it out too. He went over and gave Patches a final pat, and Patches thumped his tail and licked Jack's fingers. "I'll see you soon," promised Jack.

He went the few metres to his own house, feeling as though he was walking on air. It was true, what Jo had told him that very morning.

God had sorted things out in a wonderful way he'd never have been able to think of for himself. God had known what to do all the time, and how to do it. "Thank you, God," he whispered, as he let himself in at the door.

Inside, it was all noise and bustle as the girls got themselves ready for the evening service and youth group. The air was full of the sound of shrieking and the smell of hair spray. He was not popular.

"You made us late, having to come looking for you," said Amy.

"You never stop and think!" said Rosie.

"Anyway, there's hardly any tea left for you," said Marianne.

"And serves you right!" said Megan.

It was all quite familiar. Mum and Dad were upstairs, getting ready. The cats were under the dresser, lying low until things got quieter. Sam was in the kitchen, drying dishes. He'd saved some sandwiches and a piece of cake for Jack.

"All right, mate?" he asked.

Jack nodded, his mouth full of ham sandwich. It was all right. He'd got over being scared of the bullies, and had made friends with them. He was home with all his family, and two doors along, a young dog with brown patches waited for him to come back. His dog.

Everything was all right.

*If you've enjoyed this book, why not look
out for these other titles?*

By the same author:
Who invented sisters?
Eleanor Watkins

Jack has four sisters who boss him around.
He wonders if God made a mistake when he
put him into this family. Another warm,
funny story about the family from *Cats, Dogs
& Sisters*.

ISBN 1 85999 545 4

There's a grandad in my soup
Hilary Hawkes

Danny's grandad is an inventor. Sometimes
his inventions are very useful; sometimes they
cause chaos in the family's restaurant. Danny
wishes he were good at something and decides
to try for the Yummy Pudding Award. But the
result is not what he expected.

ISBN 1 85999 414 8

The Friend-Finding Formula
Janet Slater Bottin

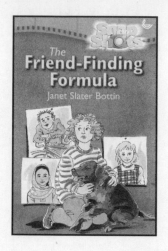

Shy Holly has no real friends. Then her gran
challenges her with the friend-finding formula.
Holly accepts the challenge to make friends
with three unlikely children in her class – an
outcast, an enemy and an outsider – and then
wishes she hadn't. But there's no backing out.

ISBN 1 85999 508 X

*You can buy these books at your local Christian
bookshop, or online at
www.scriptureunion.org.uk/publishing
or call Mail Order direct: 01908 856006*